Y0-DXC-363

Text Copyright @ 2018 by Kenyatta Scott

Illustrations Copyright @2018 by Kenyatta Scott

First paperback edition in this format 2018.

ISBN: 978-6845-879-8

To My Sister, Shante:

I was so happy to find out that pizza is your favorite food too! Thank you so much for supporting The Violet Book Series! You help me out at all "Violet" related events at the drop of a hat.

Thank you for all of your love and encouragement. I look forward to our next pizza party, courtesy of Violet!

Love,
Your "Favorite Sister"

VIOLET MAKES A PIZZA

By: Kenyatta Scott
Illustrated by: Michelle Valenta

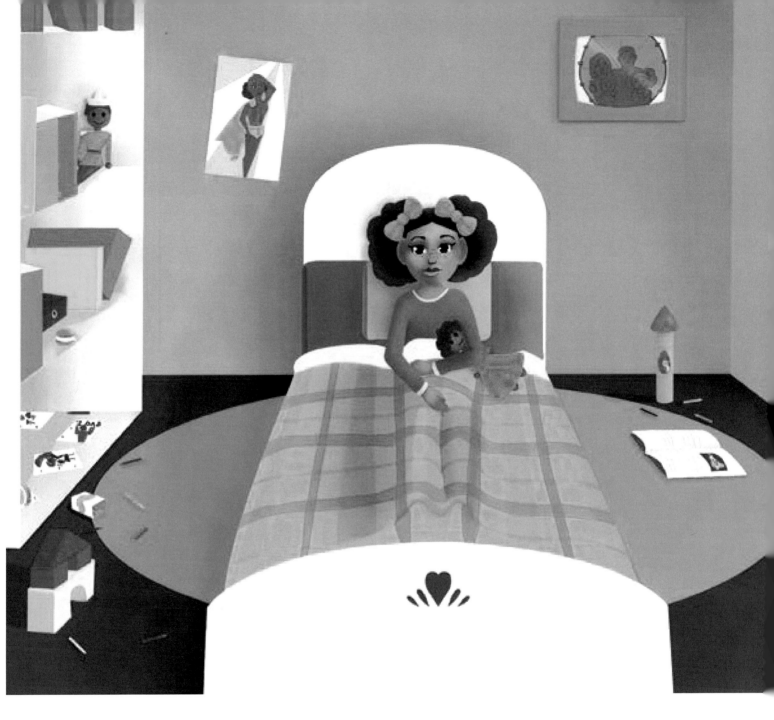

Violet woke up, excited! Today was the day that she and Daddy were going to make dinner for Stepmommy and Derek.

She was ready to go to the grocery store with Daddy to get everything they needed to cook.

Daddy is such a good cook! He said the things they were going to buy were called Ingredients. He said you put all the ingredients together and that is how you make one meal.

Violet was amazed. She did not know how hard Daddy or Stepmommy worked to make meals, like breakfast, lunch, or dinner. All she knew was that she enjoyed the eating part!

Violet sat up in bed, thinking about what food she wanted to make. Daddy said she could decide.

She thought about her favorite foods; chocolate chip pancakes, strawberry french toast, and pizza.

"Aha! Everyone in the family loves pizza!", she thought.

Derek loves cheese pizza, Stepmommy loves pineapples on her pizza, and Daddy loves pepperoni pizza.

"I think those are what Daddy calls ingredients!", Violet said to herself.

Violet got out of her bed and walked into the bathroom to get dressed to go to the grocery store.

She tried to tiptoe around the house as quietly as possible, so that she would not wake up Derek.

Soon, Violet was all dressed and ready to go. She asked Daddy if he was ready and he was! Daddy told Stepmommy that they would be back soon.

Violet smiled when they got to the door, happy that they were
on their way.

Violet looked out the window while Daddy drove them to the grocery store.

Daddy parked the car. Daddy said that she could push the cart as long as she did not bump into anyone. Violet promised him that she would be careful.

They walked the aisles, putting all of the "ingredients" inside the cart. Daddy told her which one's to get. They had pizza dough, cheese, sauce, pineapples, and pepperoni circles.

Just seeing the pizza ingredients made her even more excited! She was doing a "happy dance" inside her head.

She was excited to eat!

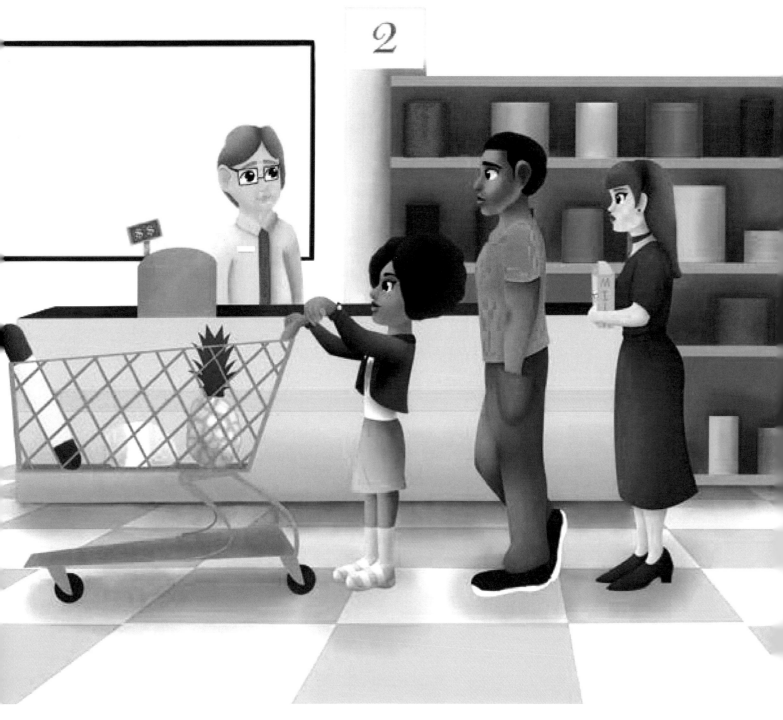

Violet pushed the cart up to the register to pay for their items.

There was a lady, with a carton of milk in her hands, waiting behind them in line. Violet watched as Daddy asked the lady if she wanted to go in front of them.

The lady smiled, thanked Daddy, went in front of them in line, and paid for her carton of milk. Then it was Violet's turn.

The cashier placed the pizza ingredients in a bag and Daddy let Violet carry the bag to the car.

Violet couldn't stop thinking to herself, "Why did Daddy let the lady go in front of us at the grocery store?" They were driving home now so Violet asked Daddy.

She pushed and pulled at the dough. She piled on lots of sauce and then, the cheese.

She put extra cheese on Derek's side of the pizza and extra pineapples on Stepmommy's side. Her and Daddy had lots of cheese and pepperoni on their side. Daddy said she did a very good job.

Now it was time for the pizza to go in the oven. Violet could hardly wait. She watched the pizza cooking in the oven. She could smell the pizza.

Her mouth watered. It was almost ready! Violet cleaned up her toys and asked Daddy if she could help him wash the dishes while the pizza was baking.

Stepmommy and Derek arrived home right as Daddy was taking the pizza out of the oven.

Violet wanted to help Daddy so she put the plates on the table.
It was time to eat!

Violet asked Derek if she could help him with cutting his pizza. Daddy smiled so big, watching them.

Everyone was laughing, talking, and eating their pizza. Stepmommy said that her and Derek would clean up after because she could tell that Violet and Daddy worked hard today.

Violet was getting sleepy now.

Stepmommy was right, she did work hard today! It was almost time for bed.

Daddy walked over to Violet as she sat on the couch. He bent down and said, "Thank you for being my little helper today, Violet.

You are so thoughtful!"

Violet was happy, inside. She whispered back, "You're welcome, Daddy." Today was a great day, after all.

Violet's Pepperoni Pizza Recipe

1 Container of Pizza Crust Dough

1 Package of Pepperoni Slices

1 Can of Cut Pineapples

1 Package of Shredded Mozzarella

1 Can of Pizza Sauce

Pre-Heat Oven to 425 Degrees

Roll Dough into a Circle on Pizza Pan

Spoon lots of Sauce on the Dough

Sprinkle Mozzarella Cheese on the Sauce

Place Pepperoni and sprinkle Pineapple Slices on Top

Bake Pizza for 13 Minutes

Eat and . . . .

Be Thoughtful like Daddy

Don't forget to share with up to 10 people !!

Conversation Questions

1. Violet is "thoughtful" 5 times in the story.
Can you find the 5 times?

2. What is the last "thoughtful" thing you said or did?

3. Violet's favorite food is pizza. What is yours?

www.thevioletbookseries.com

About the Author

Kenyatta is from the Windy City, also known as Chicago, IL. She has four sisters and two brothers. She is a Speech Therapist and Motivational Speaker. In her free time, Kenyatta loves to play with her dog, Cole. She blends her love of travel with her favorite food whenever she travels to Venice, Italy. Kenyatta is excited to share the adventures of Violet and her little brother, Derek, with you!

For Violet and Derek clothing and books, visit

www.thevioletbookseries.com

CPSIA information can be obtained
at www.ICGtesting.com
Printed in the USA
LVRC020320091219
639844LV00005B/44

* 9 7 8 1 6 8 4 5 4 8 7 9 8 *

Today starts off like any other day for Violet. Then, she remembers, she's making a pizza today! Follow along as Violet goes on a small adventure with Daddy, as she learns what it means to be "thoughtful".

Don't forget to think about, how can YOU can be thoughtful today?

ISBN 978-1-68454-879-8
90000
9 781684 548798

Trip To The Building

Written by James Morris Jr.

Illustrated By Tyrus Goshay